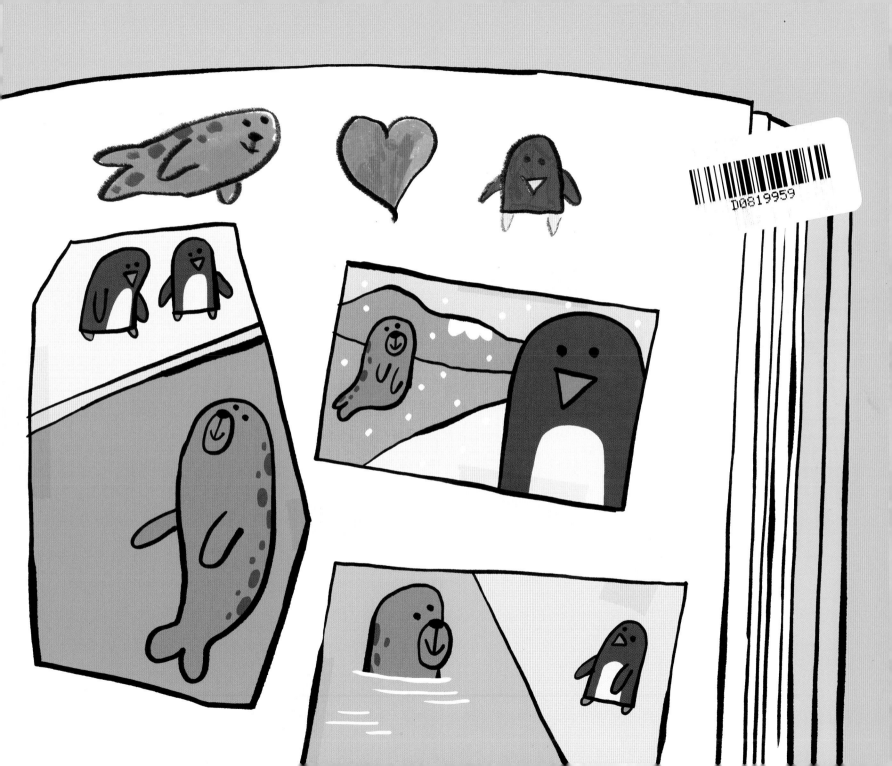

For the real Lorelei,
who inspired this story.
For her teacher, Christie Hammond,
who told it to me.
And for Rebecca Sherman,
who said I should make it a book.
— J.C.

All rights reserved. Published by Orchard Books, an imprint of Scholastic Inc., *Publishers since 1920.* ORCHARD BOOKS and design are registered trademarks of Watts Publishing Group, Ltd., used under license. SCHOLASTIC and associated logos are trademarks and/or registered trademarks of Scholastic Inc.

Library of Congress Cataloging-in-Publication Data available

ISBN 978-1-338-83568-7
10 9 8 7 6 5 4 3 2 1   23 24 25 26 27

Printed in China   62
First edition, September 2023
The text type was set in Bryant. The display type was hand lettered by Jared Chapman.
The illustrations were created digitally in Photoshop.

als Are Jerks!

Jared Chapman

Orchard Books
an imprint of Scholastic Inc.
New York

Lorelei loved seals.

They were her favorite animal for a number of reasons.

Reasons I ♥ Seals

- Big adorable eyes
- Goofy bark
- Shapeless-yet-potato-like body
- Blubber

But what she loved most was how seals and penguins were friends.

In every seal photo she had ever seen, there was a penguin nearby. She liked to imagine all the fun things they did together, and it always made her smile.

That was what she was explaining to her class when the new student interrupted her.

No, seals are jerks.

Pardon?

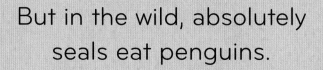

Is that Randy?
I thought he was
studying abroad.

Antarctica may have been the coldest place on Earth,
but Lorelei was hot and demanding answers.

Hey you, SEAL!
Do you eat penguins?

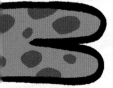

Seal could see that he wasn't getting off so easily.

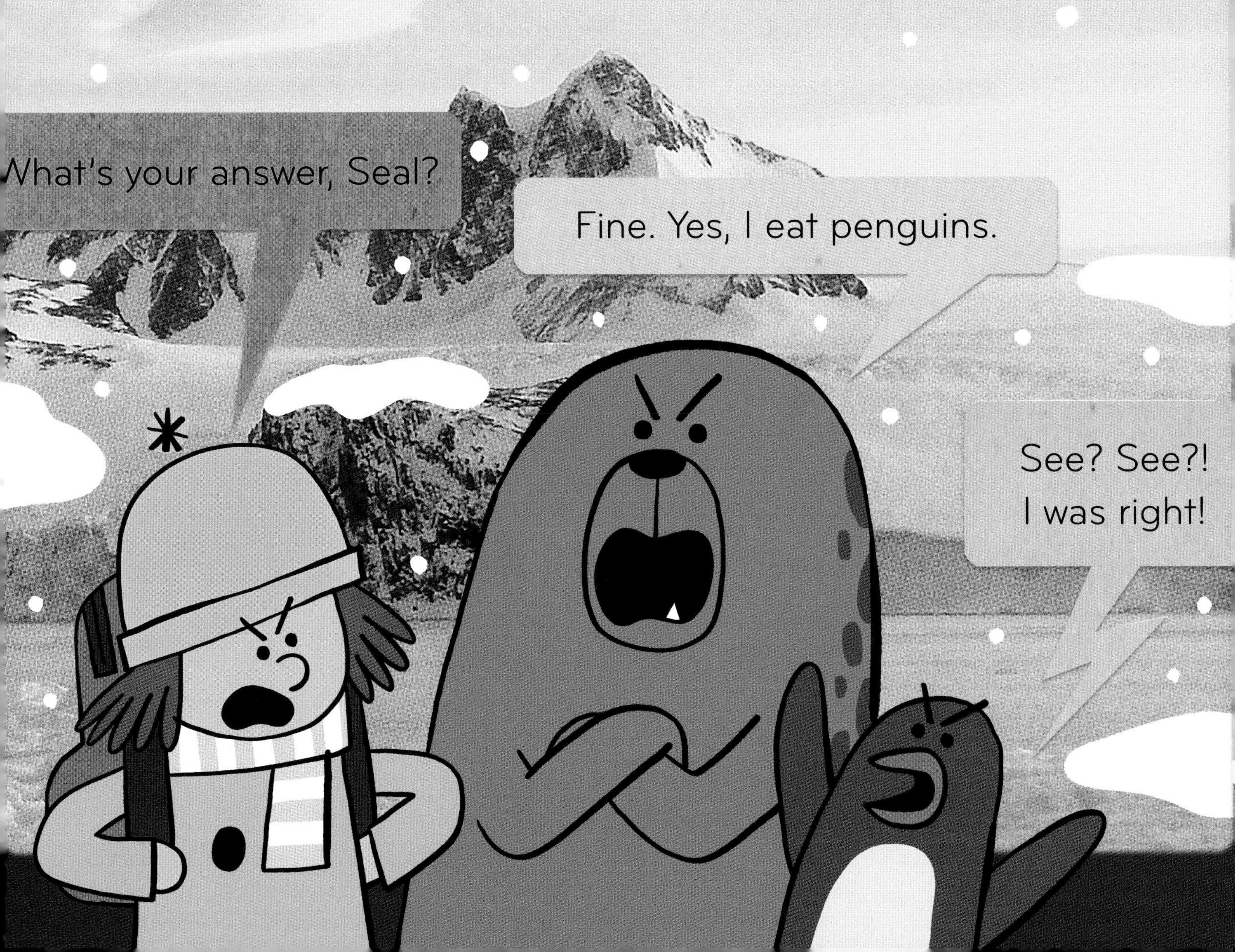

Lorelei got very quiet.

Lorelei was crushed.
She tried reasoning with Seal.

But penguins are so small and cute and helpless!

She tried offering other solutions to help smooth things over.

Have you tried other things? Meditation? Exercise? PB&Js?! They're delicious.

Regardless of what Lorelei said,
Seal could not be convinced.
She finally got it.

She wanted nothing to do with them.

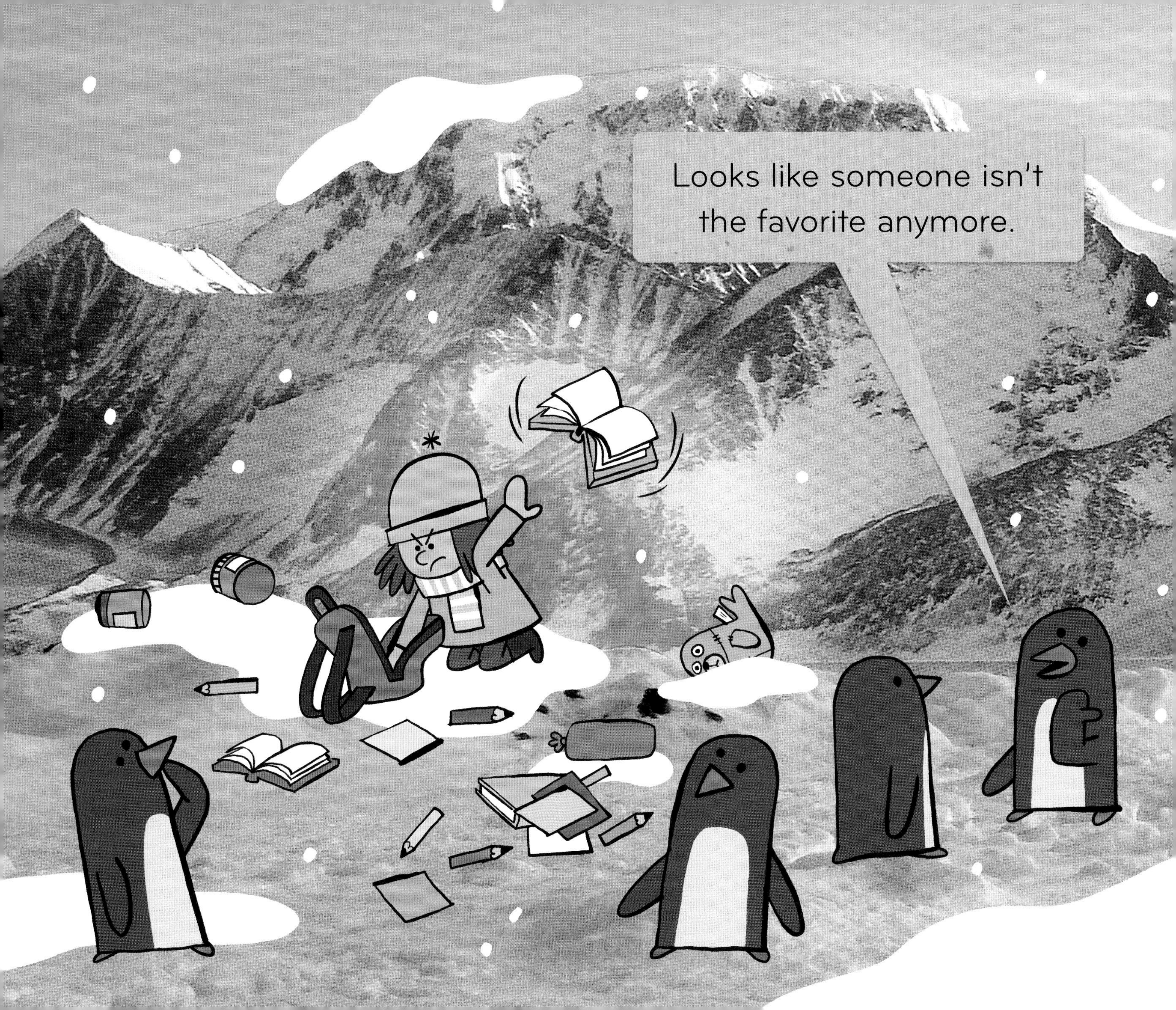
Looks like someone isn't
the favorite anymore.

Seal felt so misunderstood.

Lorelei couldn't believe what she was hearing.
She felt hopeless.

Is everyone a jerk?

It doesn't mean that I have to stop being your favorite, right?

Lorelei thought to herself for a moment.

And decided that it did not.

Hey! This is pretty good.
I mean, it's not the best
thing I've ever had, but —
Seal?
Yes?

Facts about Antarctica:

- Antarctica contains about 70 percent of Earth's fresh water and about 90 percent of its fresh water is ice. That's a lot of water.

- Are you an avid meteorite hunter? Then Antarctica is the place for you! Because everything is covered in white ice, the dark rocks are really easy to spot.

- Ever wonder what is under that thick layer of ice that covers Antarctica? Lakes! About 200 of them! I'm not even joking. The biggest, Lake Vostok, is a freshwater lake and is roughly the size of Lake Ontario.

- Can you guess what the most common bird in Antarctica is? That's right! Penguins! I mean, when they aren't studying abroad, of course.

- Did you know that there are seventeen species of penguins but only one species lives above the Southern Hemisphere? I really hope they have pen pals.

- Know why some penguins are black and white? It's the perfect camouflage from predators when they are swimming in the ocean.

- Leopard seals get their name from the spots on their coat.

- In addition to penguins, leopard seals also eat birds and shellfish.

- Since they only have ear canals, leopard seals are considered earless seals, which means they have to work really hard to be good listeners.

- The only predator of leopard seals are orcas, which makes me wonder if they have tried peanut butter and jelly sandwiches yet.